ANDRO, THIS IS CRAZY

JACK LAWSON, a teacher of communications, lives in Kingston, New York.

ANDRO, THIS IS CRAZY

JACK LAWSON

Illustrated by B. Perry White

AN AVON  CAMELOT BOOK

ANDRO, THIS IS CRAZY is an original publication of Avon Books. This work has never before appeared in book form.

AVON BOOKS
A division of
The Hearst Corporation
1350 Avenue of the Americas
New York, New York 10019

Copyright © 1991 by John Lawson
Illustrations copyright © 1991 by Avon Books
Published by arrangement with the author
Library of Congress Catalog Card Number: 91-91778
ISBN: 0-380-76234-X
RL: 3.7

First Avon Camelot Printing: July 1991

CAMELOT TRADEMARK REG. U.S. PAT. OFF. AND IN OTHER COUNTRIES, MARCA RE-GISTRADA, HECHO EN U.S.A.

Printed in the U.S.A.

OPM 10 9 8 7 6 5 4 3 2

For Jeremy,
who helped,
and for Michelle and Gregory,
who will in awhile

A Glow from the Sky

I was walking home and thinking about things. Everything was wrong. I wasn't scoring any points in basketball, and everybody else was making about ten a game. I hadn't hit a baseball since I was about four and my dad threw it practically into my bat. I tried out for the school play and got a part as a guy in the crowd. I didn't have even one line.

At school, in fact, nothing was right. I wasn't passing anything at all. The way it was going, I would be in grammar school forever. I figured: I am an *F* kind of a student when it comes to school—anything at school.

Everybody knew it, too. Because there was this guy Hennerly at school who was always pointing out all my screwups. I mean, whenever Mrs. Luff called on me to give an answer to a question, I gave it wrong. That was bad enough. But then Hennerly had to put up his hand and yell: "I know!" And he did. Then he'd give the answer and grin at me, and everybody would laugh.

He was a whiz at basketball, too. If anybody was crazy enough to throw the ball to me, Hennerly would run over and catch it instead and go down the court with it. He'd usually sink it, too. Then he'd turn and shout at me: "Thanks, Bean!" And then I could see all the guys making funny remarks about me. I hated that.

He also got a part in the school play—with lines. He was a big deal, and he never let me forget it. Not that I could, even if he didn't talk about it all the time.

So I was walking home and thinking about all that. It was late in the afternoon; I was near the edge of town, and I saw this glow. It started to lower in from the sky, like a spaceship. Well, I thought, if I am seeing a spaceship, I am probably going crazy too, with all the other things.

But I watched the glow, just to see how crazy I was. And things got worse. It's bad enough to see a glow come in and land, but if you see two men get out of it, you have to be really nuts. And if you are completely nuts, they will be beings from another planet. And that's what they were.

So I rubbed my head, and I said to myself: "You are some kind of nut, Bean, because that can't possibly be a spaceship with people getting out of it." But there they were. I figured I had finally and totally gone nuts.

"Walk on by it, Bean," I said to myself. "It's bad enough if you see it, but to go up and start talking to the space guys is enough for somebody to tie you up and take you off. They would say: 'Poor Bean. We thought it would happen sooner or later. It's on account of those games.'"

The games were baseball, where it was

my luck to get hit with the ball about every other time I came to bat. And that's why the guys started calling me Bean. I figured, all I had to do was tell everybody that I saw this glow land and guys get out of it, and everybody would say I had finally gone off my nut on account of all those bean balls.

So I walked on by. I even whistled to show that I hadn't noticed a single thing. As far as I was concerned, there was no glow there. And there weren't two guys talking. And the tall guy wasn't pointing off toward the town. And the thin guy wasn't smiling and nodding.

Then the tall guy pointed at me. When that happened, I couldn't even keep whistling. It was very hard to act like he wasn't pointing at me when he was.

The thin guy smiled and nodded and waved at me. How was I supposed to pretend *that* wasn't happening? Well, I looked around, and nobody was watching, so I waved back. I mean, a kid's got to have some manners *once* in a while.

The thin guy—the one who had waved—started talking with the tall one again and smiling and nodding at him, and I just stood there and watched. I couldn't have moved if I had wanted to.

The tall guy handed the thin guy a bunch of papers and patted him on the shoulder. Then a funny thing happened. The tall guy got in the glow, and the glow started rising. The thin guy was still on the ground! He even waved at the glow as it went. I mean, he didn't call after it like it had forgotten him or anything! He only smiled at it and waved and watched it go up until it became so small that I couldn't see it anymore. And then the thin guy was next to me—without walking or anything! He was just there.

I thought: *Now* what do I do? I can't very well just walk off and pretend that the guy wasn't there, when I'd just waved at him. You don't wave at things and then say they weren't there in the first place. If you do that, you probably deserve to be taken off. So I just stood there.

The guy said to me, "Hi! My name is Andro. What did you learn in the first grade? I am doing a survey."

What kind of a way is *that* to start a conversation? How do I know what I learned in the first grade? Nothing, the way I have been going lately. I just stood there. I didn't know what to say. This is some kind of a strange guy, I thought.

He didn't *look* very strange, though. His hair was a little wild, as if he hadn't combed it in quite a while, and his eyes had that sparkle that people's eyes get when they're having a lot of fun. Otherwise, he looked pretty much like any other guy.

"You mustn't let me confuse you," he said. "I am probably too quick for you. I do forget at times how very quick I am. Let's start over. What is your name?"

Well, that was better. I still didn't know who this guy was or where he was from, but it wouldn't hurt to tell him my name. "Bean," I said. "But that isn't my real name. That's the name they gave me because I was always getting beaned with a baseball."

"Interesting," he said. "In my world, we are beyond that. Oh, much beyond that. My name is Andro, and they call me Andro. They do not call me something else. Ah, but your world is not as advanced as ours. I must make a note of that."

He spent quite a while leafing through the forms he had, and I started to think of ways I could get out of there. This was getting a little crazy.

"Very well," the guy said. "I have made a note. And a very interesting note it is. Now! Shall we proceed?"

"I think I'd better be getting home," I said.

"Of course," he said.

And then what happened next I couldn't believe. Because without moving—or even having time to think about moving—there we were in my room.

That was impossible. I looked around. It

was my room, all right. "How did we get here?" I said.

"How?" said Andro. "We thought our way here. How else would we get here?"

"I usually walk," I said.

2

Andro Settles In

"I had completely forgotten," Andro said. "You still walk here. How delightfully primitive! I must make a note." And he fumbled with his papers. "Now, where shall I put it? Under classroom size? No, of course not. And it won't go under age graduated from third grade."

He kept flipping the pages over. Then he said: "Hah! Here! Miscellaneous! Best place in the world to put things that are—shall we say—miscellaneous, don't you think? Advanced as we are in my world, we have still kept 'miscellaneous.' Isn't that interesting?"

"I guess," I said.

"Now, what you should understand," he said, "is that we on my planet are quite interested in educational systems on other planets, particularly the less advanced ones. I have been assigned to earth. Do you understand?"

I nodded. "Sort of."

"You'll understand oh, so much better tomorrow when I do my research. You may watch me, firsthand. Isn't that splendid?"

"I can't," I said. "I have to go to school."

"Ah, but so do I. *That's* my research—to go to school with you and discover how your educational system works. I'll be no bother. I'll simply float around here and there. Perhaps I'll assume a form or two. I sometimes do that, you know. Oh, I may assume the form of the principal, perhaps, and snoop about. I learn some marvelous things that way."

This was getting to be too much. I wouldn't mind answering questions for this guy, but I wasn't about to take him to school with me. Not if he was going to float around all over the place. Can you imagine how long I would last, taking something like him to school?

"No," I said. "You can't go to school with me. I mean, things are bad enough at school as it is."

"Ah!" he said. "Then I will make them better. What would you like me to do? Pass your tests for you? Make you a basketball star?"

"No. I would like you to stay here. I can take your forms to school with me and fill them out for you."

"Oh, no!" he said. "That would never do! You could never fill them out. Only a very advanced mind can do that. No, I really must go to school with you. But I won't embarrass you. I'll stay very much in the background, just hovering about, you know?"

"I wish you'd pick somebody else," I said. "How about a guy I know in my class? His name is Hennerly. He'd be a great guy for you. He could show you all over the place. He's a big deal. He's in the school play, too.

He's a rotten actor—I mean, really bad—but he could tell you as much as I can. Not any more, really, but probably as much."

"Oh, no," Andro said. "No, that would not do, I fear. I am not permitted to pick and choose. We have rules, you know. We must go to the very first person we see. That makes it fair, you know. If we didn't do it that way, there would be so many clamoring at us to be interviewed! Oh, it would be too much!"

"It would be all right with me," I said.

But he wasn't paying any attention to what I wanted. What *he* wanted was what mattered. And what he wanted was to go to school with me.

"Okay," I said. "I guess I haven't got any choice about it. I mean, you're going to school with me, whether I want you to or not."

"You'll love it," he said.

Yeah, I thought. I'll bet.

"Not a soul will even know who I am," he said. "Because, you see, I couldn't tell anyone, even if I wanted to. We can tell one person only. And that person is you. It's too bad in a way. Think of how many people are denied the wonder of knowing us. But that is the rule."

"You're pretty sure of yourselves on your planet, aren't you?" I said. "I mean, you're not modest or anything."

"Modest?" he said. "Oh, indeed we are! But confident too, you know. A person must be convinced of his worth, don't you think?"

"I guess."

"And now," he said, "according to my notes, your dinnertime is near. You do still eat on your planet, don't you? Or am I thinking of Moltar?"

"No," I said. "You're thinking of us. We eat dinner."

"Excellent. Of course! I knew I was right. Your mother is about to call you now, in fact."

And before I had a chance to say anything, my mother called me. "Jefferson? Dinnertime!"

"Jefferson?" Andro said, looking at me.

"Yeah," I said. "Wouldn't you want to be called Bean, even on your planet, if your name was Jefferson?"

"Names are very important on any planet," Andro said. "We carry them with us to the grave."

"Yeah, that's where mine belongs," I said.

"Then I shall call you Bean. But, of course, I must enter your real name on my forms."

"How about lying on the forms?" I said. "I mean, Bean's the name I want, and that's what counts, isn't it? And if some other planet is going to hear about me, I'd just as soon they didn't know my real name."

"Ah," said Andro, "but we never lie on our planet. We are beyond that, you know. Besides, I think Jefferson is a splendid name."

"Jefferson!" my mother called.

"Coming," I yelled.

"Good-bye, Bean," Andro said. "I'll be waiting."

I nodded. It was only my luck. Nothing had gone right yet. Why should I expect it to now? But then I thought of one thing.

"Andro?" I said.

"Yes, my boy?"

"If it's all right with you, I'll just *walk* on down to dinner."

3

"I'll Be Very Clever"

Dinner was the usual thing. My sister, Doreen, talked the whole time about things that weren't the least bit important—I mean no matter how you looked at them.

My dad didn't say much. How could he? No one could get a word in at all. And my mother spent most of her time telling my little brother that he had to keep his food on his plate, because you weren't supposed to eat off the table.

So I was just sitting there eating, thinking about what a mess it would be in school tomorrow with Andro floating around in people's forms and how I would get blamed for it. And then I heard this thing in my mind. It wasn't a sound, like the kind you hear from outside. I knew it was *inside* my head. It said: *Bean? Oh, Bean?*

I looked at my mother, but she was arguing with my little brother. My sister was still talking away. So I knew no one heard. I just ignored it.

But it came again. *Bean? Come up here, will you? It will take only a minute.*

Now, that is something to happen to you! Right in the middle of dinner, a guy from outer space calls you and tells you to come upstairs. What was I supposed to say to my mother? "Excuse me. A spaceman is calling?"

And then the voice came again: *Bean? You really must come up here! I need an answer, or I shall be terribly behind in my forms.*

I figured I'd better run up. Before he floated down. So I said: "Excuse me, please. I have to go to the bathroom." And I left the table and started upstairs.

"Jefferson?" my mother said. "What is

the matter with you? The bathroom isn't upstairs."

"The bathroom?" I said. "Did I say bathroom? I meant bedroom. I have to go and get a handkerchief." But my mother just looked at me like something was goofy. "I can't very well use the napkin," I said.

She shrugged and turned back to my brother. "Stanley! *Get* those potatoes off the table!"

So I was clear, and I ran up to my room. Andro was sitting at my desk. There were papers all over the place. "What would you say your form of government is?" he said. "Universal democratic constitutional or statutory liberated monarchical?"

"Does it have to be one or the other?" I said.

"Well, I certainly think it *should* be."

"I think it's democratic," I said. "Or republican. Or maybe both."

Andro scratched his head. "That does pose a problem. Are you sure it's not either of the ones I mentioned?"

"I don't think so," I said.

"Oho!" he said. "I've got it! We'll say it's miscellaneous! What would we do without miscellaneous?"

I went back down to dinner, and I could hear him humming to himself as he went on with his forms.

"Were you talking up there?" my mother said as I sat down.

"Uh . . . yeah," I said. "I was running over some lines from the play."

"Oh," my mother said. "But I thought you didn't have any lines."

"I decided to give myself some."

After dinner, I went back up to my room, but Andro wasn't there. Great! I thought. He's probably down in the kitchen floating around. That's all I needed—for my mother to call me down and ask me if I brought in that thing that is floating around in the kitchen.

"Well! You're back!" said Andro. I looked around, but I couldn't see him. I looked under the bed and in the closet. But he wasn't there either. "Oh!" he said. "I forgot! You can't see me!" And then he appeared. Just like that. All of a sudden, he was there.

"You know," I said, "I don't see how you're going to go to school with me and not end up in detention or something. I don't think you ought to go. You're always doing things that people at school are going to think are pretty crazy."

"Ah, but no one will even know I'm there," he said. "I'll be very clever."

"I wish I could believe that," I said. "The way I see it, tomorrow is going to be a disaster."

"Ah, but you must think positively, my boy. Think, and it will be."

"I *am* thinking," I said, "and it probably will be. That's what I'm afraid of."

4

Relaxing a Little

"You must think of it this way," An-dro said. "You will go to school tomorrow, and I will be there in the same room, taking notes and notes and notes on my forms. But no one will see me. And when your teacher asks you a question, I will tell you the answer. And you will give it. And it will be the right one. The questions on earth are so simple, you know. We learned them years and years ago. In kindergarten, I think. Or nursery school."

I thought about that. In a way, it would be kind of great. Hennerly thinks he's so smart in math. And maybe he is. But he doesn't have to tell everybody about it, does he?

It's like the play. Hennerly's part in that

is big. And he is really bad. But does he let anyone forget that he got the part? Not Hennerly! And in math, he's even worse. Because he makes a fool out of me.

I looked at Andro. "Would I be able to give the right answers in math?"

"As simple as *that!*" Andro snapped his fingers.

"Hmmm. How about science?"

"Any question at all. You will answer it."

"That'll surprise them," I said.

"Fine. Now, get out your homework, and I'll show you. It'll be oh, so simple. You'll see."

"I can't," I said. "I have play practice in a half hour. Tomorrow is Thursday, and that's the night of the play. It's dress rehearsal tonight."

"Oh? What is a play?"

"You don't know what a play is?"

"No. Is it fun? What do you play?"

"We don't play, exactly," I said. "We act out a story."

"Aha. I understand. And what is the story about?"

"Well," I said, "it's about this guy called Rip van Winkle, who goes to sleep for twenty years and then wakes up. And there's a crowd of people in it, and I'm in the crowd."

"It sounds splendid," Andro said. "Shall I go?"

"No!" I said. "Plays don't have anything to do with school. Well, they have to do with school, but they're after school. They're not a class or anything."

"Fine," Andro said. "In that case, there'll be no need for me to go. I'll stay here and rest. I'll need much rest, you know. Those of us in the universe who are all mind must keep our minds in shape." He looked at me, puzzled. "You do not understand me, do you?"

"No," I said.

"Well," he said, "I shall explain it to you. We are nothing but mind, you see. My body is not really here at all. I create it with my mind because you here on earth, poor things that you are, think a person should have one. I can change it into something else if you like. How about an ostrich?"

And all of a sudden he was an ostrich. In my room!

"If you come to school with me tomorrow," I said, "do not come like that."

"How about a box of oranges?" And there, on the floor, was a box of oranges. And then he was himself again. "Don't worry," he said. "When we do our investigations—as I will be doing tomorrow—we usually assume only the forms of people."

"That's a relief," I said. I opened the closet and got out my coat. "Well, I'll go to play practice."

He looked at me, and his eyes kind of glowed, and I knew what he was thinking. "No," I said. "My dad takes me. We're going to *drive* there."

"Oh, well, have it your way," Andro said. He returned to his forms. Then he looked up. "Have a good play practice. I'm sure you'll do splendidly."

"Yeah," I said. "Well, good-bye. And by the way, it would not be a good idea to float around the kitchen downstairs, because my mother is kind of funny about things like that."

"Oh, dear me," Andro said. "I wouldn't dream of upsetting your mother."

5

Off to School

Play practice went okay. Hennerly botched up a couple of his lines. I didn't botch up mine, but then I didn't have any.

When I got back to my room, Andro was stretched out asleep. I stood there, staring at him. It was crazy. I closed the door as fast as I could, and he opened his eyes. "I thought I'd rest here," he said, "in the bed above yours. Bunk beds are so cozy, don't you think?"

"I don't *have* bunk beds," I said. "There *is* no bed above mine."

He leaned over and looked. "So there isn't," he said. He was suspended in mid-air. "Well," he said, "I don't need one anyway. We just stretch out someplace, you know, and rest. Rest is very important if the mind is to function properly."

I put my coat in the closet and went over to the desk to do my homework. But it was done! There were answers all over the place. Not like my work, where I get about one answer to every fifty questions—and then it's wrong.

"Math is so terribly simple," Andro said.

"Sure," I said.

"Hop off to sleep," he said. "Tomorrow is an important day. If you *think* it's going to be fine, it will. You'll see."

I got in bed, and it was pretty hard getting to sleep. With a guy from outer space suspended above you in the air like that, with his hands behind his head, like there was a pillow there, which there wasn't, how could anybody get to sleep?

I thought about all the terrible things that would probably happen at school tomorrow. Then I tried thinking that everything would be fine, in case Andro was right that thinking would make it happen. But I

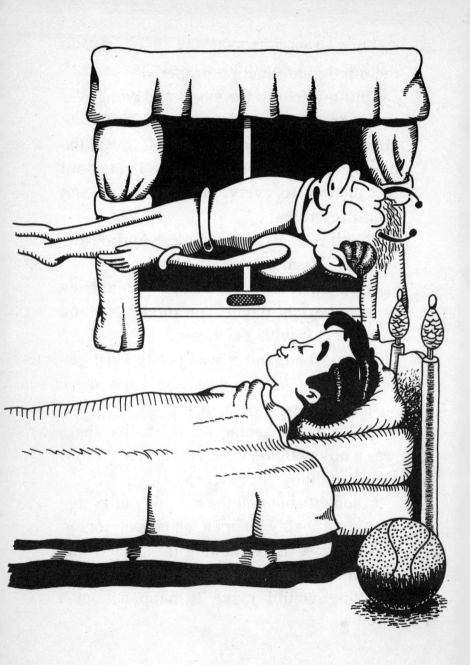

couldn't figure out any way in the world that everything could be fine. Pretty soon that wore me out, and I fell asleep.

The next thing I knew, it was morning, and Andro was over at the desk, puttering around with his papers. "Forms, forms, forms!" he was saying.

I sat up in bed.

"Good morning," he said, still getting his forms in order. "Are you feeling refreshed?"

"I don't know," I said. "I guess so."

"Of course you are! It will be a marvelous day. You'll see."

I didn't see much hope of that, but I got up and went down to the bathroom and took a shower.

"Have your breakfast. I'll just work on my forms," Andro said after I came back up and got dressed.

"Okay," I said. And I went down to the breakfast table and nibbled for a while, and my mother asked me why I wasn't eating anything. "I guess I'm a little nervous about the play tonight," I said.

"Yes," my mother said. "I can understand that." I wished she could understand what I understood.

And so we took off for school. Andro was in a hurry to get going with his study and wanted to think our way there. But I told him that would get us there a half hour early, and nothing would be happening yet.

"Very well," he said. "We will enjoy the scenery, then." So we started off to school, walking. It was October, and the leaves were starting to turn. There was frost on the ground. "Very lovely," he said. "I must make a note of that. Your trees are very lovely on earth."

And then he said, "What is *that?*"

I didn't see anything, only a dog trotting along, going nowhere in a big hurry, like dogs always do.

"That!" he said. And he pointed to the dog.

"It's a dog," I said.

"How exciting! I've never seen one be-fore. I've seen many animals—spordos and angwelts and the usual thing you see every-where—but I've never seen a dog! This is, indeed, an interesting planet." And he watched the dog until it disappeared into the woods.

When we got to school, kids were com-ing from all over the place and talking and hurrying to their lockers. I said, "You know, it's not going to look so good with you following me everywhere."

"Of course!" he said and disappeared. "Is that better?"

"Well, I'm not sure if it is or not," I said. I looked around to see if anyone had seen him disappear. No one was paying any at-tention to us. Everyone was too busy rush-ing into school.

"Also," I said, "it's better if you don't talk, because people here are not used to voices that come from nowhere."

"Yes," his voice said. And then I heard in my mind: *I mean, yes.*

So I walked along, trying to look normal—trying to look like a guy who was walking along without an invisible man from outer space behind him. And I thought I was doing pretty well until a guy named Jimbo came up to me and said, "Bean! What's the matter? You look awful!"

"What do you mean, what's the matter?" I said. "Nothing's the matter. Who said anything was the matter?"

"Nobody. You just looked so funny. Like someone was chasing you or something."

"Well, that is the dumbest thing I've heard all day," I said.

"Okay!" Jimbo said. "Sorry I mentioned it."

Actually, Jimbo is a good guy, and I liked him. He was playing Rip van Winkle in the play, and we always had a pretty good time at rehearsals. He started to walk away, so I said, "Jimbo, wait a minute." And he stopped. "Jimbo, I feel fine. And if you think you're going to be fine, you're going to be fine."

"Okay," Jimbo said, and he walked on down the hall. Then he turned and stared at me as if I looked crazier than I had before. I thought: This is going to be some day.

6

Math—and Trouble

I went to class and sat at my desk. The bell rang, and Mrs. Luff said the usual junk and then started reading the bulletin. That was the same stuff too. She read about assemblies we were going to have and what they would be about and the other things that were going on. I kept hearing Andro in my head, saying things like: *Splendid! A very good thing to talk about,* and *Oho! That is a good idea!* and *Marvelous! I will make a note of that.* And it got so bad that I felt like saying to him: Will you keep quiet? I can't hear a thing that she's saying.

But I guess he took notes for the rest of the morning, because I didn't hear any more from him. Mrs. Luff talked the whole time about how Canada was explored by a

guy named Champlain. But I didn't pay any attention. I was thinking partly about the play and partly about how long it was going to take for school to get over. And I even forgot about Andro.

But when recess came and I was leaving the classroom, I remembered him. He said, *Quite fascinating, you know, the things that Champlain did.*

"Yeah," I said. "I know."

"What?" said a guy next to me. "You say something to me?"

"No," I said. "I'm in the play tonight. I was just practicing my lines."

"Yeah?" the guy said. "Is it going to be good?"

"Sure," I said.

"You got a lot of lines?"

"Uh—no."

"How many?"

"None," I said.

The guy looked at me kind of funny and walked off.

I got back to class and took the math

homework out of my book and put it on my desk and sat down.

Mrs. Luff was sitting at her desk. When the bell rang, she looked at us and said, "All right. We'll begin with the exercises you did last night."

Okay, I thought, this will be one day at least when I'll get them right. Providing Andro knows math. I hope he knows what he's doing.

And then I heard in my head: *Oh, I do! It's so simple, really.*

So I just sat there and waited for Mrs. Luff to call on me. It'll be just my luck she won't today, I thought.

Some of the kids had the answers wrong. Hennerly, of course, had his hand up every time with the right answer. I thought, Wait till he hears *my* answer. It'll kill him!

Right then, Mrs. Luff called on me. "Bean," she said, "number twelve."

I looked at my paper, where Andro had the answers written. I found the answer to number twelve and read it out loud: "Two hundred seventy-eight point six."

I looked at Hennerly to see how stunned he was, but he was smiling and shaking his head.

"Well," Mrs. Luff said, "congratulations, Bean. That is almost right."

Almost right! Andro's voice boomed in my head.

"The numbers are right," Mrs. Luff said, "but the decimal point should be after the seven instead of the eight." She smiled and then said: "Now, think it out. Why is that so?"

And now I was in trouble! How could I think out why that was so? I didn't even know why the numbers were right. I'm finished now, I thought.

Not at all, Andro's voice said. I looked around. Fortunately, it was only in my head.

I looked at Mrs. Luff and smiled back at her. "I—I will need a minute to think," I said.

"Of course," she said.

I thought: Andro, now what do I do?

Simply say what I tell you.

Okay, I thought. Here goes! And I said exactly what Andro told me to say: "Actually, at one time in history—when little or nothing was known of the suprasegmental aspects of base ten—it was thought that binomials would act in this fashion."

"I beg your pardon?" Mrs. Luff said. And every kid in the class was staring at me. But I just smiled.

Andro's voice said to me: *Well, we will simply rephrase it.* And so this is what he told me to say to clear things up: "On the surface, it does, indeed, seem that these integers are in a linear array. But if one simply takes into account the converse relativistic equation, one can see that they could be—but need not be—decilinear."

Everybody in the class was talking now. Mrs. Luff stood up and asked me to come forward. I did.

41

"Where did you get what you just said?" she asked me.

And I looked straight at her and said, "Out of my head." Which was true.

"It is fairly advanced for you, isn't it?"

I nodded. "Fairly."

Everybody laughed at that. I turned and smiled at them.

"Jefferson!" Mrs. Luff said. "That will be enough. Would you like to see Mr. Elbauer?"

Mr. Elbauer was the vice principal in charge of punishing kids.

And I heard Andro's voice: *That would be splendid!*

So I said, "That would be splendid!"

Everybody burst into laughter again, harder than ever, and Mrs. Luff said, "Quiet, please!" She sounded as if she was mad. Everybody shut up. "Jeanette," she said, "come up here and watch the class. Jefferson and I are going to see Mr. Elbauer." And she took me by the arm and marched me out of the room.

Mrs. Luff is actually an okay teacher. I guess she thought she had to take me, since I had said it would be splendid to see Mr. Elbauer. I didn't really think that, of course, because Mr. Elbauer is definitely *not* okay, but Andro had messed me up.

That does seem to be the way it turned out, Andro's voice said. *I'll just dash ahead and fix matters.*

Mrs. Luff and I walked down the hall, and things didn't look too good. We turned a corner into another hall and finally got to the door that was marked: A. J. ELBAUER, VICE PRINCIPAL.

Now I'm in for it, I thought, and we walked in.

Mr. Elbauer's secretary was sitting at a desk, and Mrs. Luff said to her, "We will need a few minutes of Mr. Elbauer's time."

"You can go in," the secretary said.

So we walked into Mr. Elbauer's office. I had heard plenty about this room. You really got chewed out in here. And you didn't forget it fast, either. So I clenched my teeth and thought, Well, here it comes!

Mr. Elbauer didn't look up when we came in. He was looking through some papers on his desk. "Forms, forms, forms!" he said.

Oh, oh! I thought.

Mr. Elbauer looked up. "Well, my friend," he said to Mrs. Luff, "what can I do for you?" Now, that didn't sound like Mr. Elbauer at all. Mr. Elbauer would have said, "So you've brought me another one. This one looks plenty bad!" Or something like that.

Mrs. Luff said, "Bean here was a little smart in class, and I felt he should see you. I think it would help if you would talk with him."

"Certainly," Mr. Elbauer said. "He looks plenty bad."

7

More Trouble

Well, I got out of that one okay. It turned out that Mr. Elbauer had stepped into the bathroom next to his office. Andro and I were gone by the time he came back.

While Andro and I were walking back to class, I told him I didn't want him to give me any more answers. "The ones I turn in get me into a lot less trouble," I said, "and they're wrong."

"I understand perfectly," he said, walking alongside me.

"And also," I said, "I don't think you'd better stay in Mr. Elbauer's shape too much longer. Somebody might get suspicious. And I *know* they will if we run into Mr. Elbauer."

"You're right, of course," Andro said, and he disappeared.

We got back to class, and the rest of the morning went okay, except that Andro said that most of Mrs. Luff's answers were wrong.

When lunchtime came, I started down to the cafeteria. Andro said he thought he'd go along too. He thought he would go along in his human shape so he could talk to people.

I thought that was a pretty bad idea. Visitors don't eat in the cafeteria. But Andro said it would be okay, so what could I do? I mean, Andro was from outer space. Who was I to tell him not to go in the cafeteria? Only Mr. Elbauer could do that. Even a man from outer space has to do what Mr. Elbauer says. At least that's what I thought.

So we walked into the cafeteria. No sooner had we got there than everybody started staring at us. *Now* what? I thought. I turned to Andro, and he was walking on his hands.

"It is very good for the circulation and strengthens the hand muscles, as well," he said.

"Yeah, but this is the cafeteria," I said. "Outside during recess, that's all right. In here, they call it clowning around, and you get thrown out for it."

"If you say so," Andro said, and he flipped over onto his feet, and we walked toward the line. Everybody was still looking at us, but I tried to pretend that they weren't. It is almost impossible to act like nobody is looking at you when everyone in a cafeteria *is* looking at you. And this is even more true when the vice principal comes over and starts eyeing you up and down and then glares at the guy who is with you.

Andro nodded to Mr. Elbauer and smiled. "Nice day, wouldn't you say? And a very nice cafeteria too."

Mr. Elbauer narrowed his eyes. Mr. Elbauer liked to narrow his eyes, because it made him look meaner. "We do not permit parents in the cafeteria," he said.

"That is fine," Andro said. "I am not a parent."

"We also do not allow adults."

"Well, I am not an adult either," Andro said. "Let me see, what am I? How can I put it so that a simple mind can understand? Ah! A force field! Does that ring a bell?"

By this time, Mr. Elbauer's face was turning red. Everybody in the cafeteria went back to eating, or at least pretended they were.

"I'm sorry," Mr. Elbauer said, "but you must leave."

I was sure Andro would put up a fight, but he didn't. "Very well," he said. "If I must, I must." And he was slowly becoming invisible. Everybody could see right through him! I closed my eyes. How was I going to explain that? That I came into the cafeteria with someone who was turning invisible?

But Mr. Elbauer was so angry that he must not have noticed he could see the other side of the room through Andro. All he did was sputter. "I *said* you must leave!"

"*All* the way?" Andro said.

"Yes! And now!"

"Oh, very well," Andro said, and he slowly became a mist, like a cloud. And then the mist curled into a ball and drifted up to the ceiling of the cafeteria and floated around there for a while. Mr. Elbauer stood below, pointing at the mist and shouting, "You are not putting anything over on *me!* I see you!" And then the mist was gone. There was nothing there anymore.

There wasn't a sound in the room by this time, and everyone was looking at Mr. Elbauer. He turned and scowled at them. Everyone went back to eating as fast as he could. Then Mr. Elbauer stalked out of the cafeteria without saying a word.

I got out of there as soon as I could, I can tell you. And I thought: Andro, please stay

invisible for a while—at least till after school.

And I heard his voice in my head: *You don't by chance think I should have a nice talk with Mr. Elbauer? I'm sure he would be quite fascinated.*

"No!" I said. I mean, No! I thought.

Well, he said, *off to class then!*

So we went to class. I didn't pay much attention. I was scared that Andro would do something horrible. But he didn't. Mostly, he listened.

At afternoon recess, while we were walking down the hall, he said that Mrs. Luff had it all wrong about how neutrons work. But he said she looked like a pretty bright teacher and would learn quite a bit in the next thousand years or so.

"I don't think she'll live that long," I said.

"Oh? Is she sick?"

"Nobody lives that long here."

"Well, you must learn then! It's simply a matter of using your mind, you know."

Andro and I went back to class, and the

rest of it went okay, as I said. Mrs. Luff talked about social studies. Andro didn't know anything about that, so he listened and only said *Amazing!* or *Absolutely marvelous!* once in a while. He didn't bother me much. I started thinking about gym, which was my last class.

Gym bothered me. We'd play basketball, and I would do lousy. I knew that. I was hoping that at least Hennerly wouldn't score a million points, as he usually did. Because if he did, he would talk about it all night at the play and mess up my acting.

We got out of class and went to gym. I thought: Well, at least Andro can't mess me up from here on. Things couldn't be so bad in gym.

And they weren't. They weren't bad at all. What they were was unbelievable.

Hennerly Scores
for the Wrong Team

I went into the gym and got ready for the game.

"You don't mind if I watch, do you?" Andro said. "I'll sit way up in the bleachers, where no one will notice."

"Well," I said, "if you watch, it's one thing. But if you come down here and mess things up, then I think I mind."

"I wouldn't dream of doing such a thing. I'll go and sit peaceably and watch. I won't say a word. I promise."

"Okay," I said.

So Andro sat in the bleachers, and I started warming up. Warming up for what, I didn't know—to drop the ball all over the place, I imagined. I had this talent for losing everything. I mean, you could invent a game, and I would show you how to lose it.

Well, at least I kept losing. I didn't quit.

The coach chose the teams first. He lined everyone up, and we counted off, 1-2-3-4, down the line. Everybody who was 1 or 3 was on the Green team, and the 2s and 4s were on the Red.

Hennerly ended up on the Red team, and I was on the Green. I thought: Great. I'll never get the ball.

The coach threw the ball up, and we started to play. As usual, the ball didn't get near me. But Hennerly wasn't doing that well either. There were a couple of girls on our team who kept throwing the ball right past him. When he ran after it, they'd toss it over his head. The girls were taller than he was, and that helped. Also, I don't think they liked him, because he was such a smart aleck. That was okay with me.

We played for several minutes, and nobody scored. Then this great thing happened. Somebody goofed, and the ball went bouncing down the court. I ran after it and by some miracle got it.

Well, I thought, here I go. I'll probably trip and throw the ball to Hennerly or dribble it into the parking lot, or some dumb thing like that.

I started running toward the basket, dribbling the ball, dodging all over the place. I was getting there, too.

About six feet away from the basket, a couple of guys from the Red team came running toward me. I jumped as high as I could, with the ball over my head. I was going to throw it toward the basket. I figured it'd probably go through the gym window or something.

But it wasn't like that. I've never felt anything like it. I went into the air and zoomed toward the basket, ten feet over everybody's head! And then to make things even crazier, when I got to the basket and dropped the ball in, I didn't come down. I

just stayed there. I was hanging in the air, next to the basket, feeling like an idiot.

Everybody was shouting, "Look!" I felt like the whole world was staring at me.

I looked over at Andro in the bleachers. And I heard him in my head. *You're doing quite nicely.*

Nicely! I thought. How can I be doing nicely when I'm hanging ten feet in the air?

Well, you must wait for the others, he said. *It isn't polite to go on until they've had a chance to put the ball in too.*

No! You don't understand! We throw the ball in as often as we can, and we try to keep them from throwing it in. The team that gets it in the most times wins!

Oh, Andro said. And I sank to the floor, like I was in an elevator.

"Two points for the Green team," shouted the coach.

"What kind of trick is this?" Hennerly screamed. It occurred to me that this game wasn't going too badly, after all. If it could

make Hennerly mad, there had to be something good about it.

I was walking back to my end of the
court. "What do you mean, trick?" I said.

"Where are the wires?"

"Oh, for crying out loud!" I said and went
on down the court.

"Maybe there's a wind here," he said.

The game started again, and Hennerly
was running all over the place, getting
madder and madder about my basket.

Then he got the ball, and he started toward the basket at our end. When he got
near the basket, he jumped, with the ball
over his head. And he really flew up, almost as far as I had. "Yahoo!" he shouted.
"This is some wind!" But then, he kept going up, right past the basket. Pretty soon,
he began to look a little worried.

"Throw it!" shouted some of the kids.
But before he had a chance to do that, Hennerly started drifting toward the other end
of the court.

He got red in the face. "What's going

on?" he shouted. "I'm going the wrong way! Stop!" But he kept drifting, closer and closer to the other end.

"You're supposed to be going *that* way!" the coach shouted, pointing toward the other basket.

Then I heard Andro's voice in my head: *He's quite wrong, of course. To be fair, Hennerly should throw it in the same basket you did, Bean. True?*

No, I thought. I wasn't really too upset about things. But I had to tell Andro. He's supposed to throw it in the other basket, because he's on the other team.

How stupid of me! Andro said. *I shall put him down, then.* And Hennerly drifted down toward the floor, then crashed to the ground, right on top of Buzz Andrews, who was on our side.

"Personal foul," said the coach. "Free throw for the Greens."

Hennerly jumped to his feet. "Who are you talking about?" he said.

"You," said the coach. "You're not supposed to bump into players on the other team."

"I didn't bump into him!" Hennerly said. "I dropped on top of him because of the wind."

"Looked like a personal foul to me," I said. Hennerly turned and glared at me. But I only smiled.

Everybody was talking about the wind now. It was the funniest wind anyone had ever seen. But we went on with the game.

The coach gave me the ball for the free throw. I walked to the free throw line and threw the ball, but it missed the basket.

The game got pretty furious now, because we were ahead by only two points. We were a little nervous about that. In fact, Tim Keevers was so nervous that when he got the ball, he dribbled it right out of bounds.

That meant a throw-in by the Reds, and the coach handed the ball to Ernie Waters. He immediately threw it in from the sidelines to Hennerly, who pranced around with it for a while. And then he threw the ball.

It went right for the basket, hit the rim, and spun around on it.

"Wow!" Hennerly shouted. "Two points! Game's tied!"

But the ball didn't go into the basket. It just kept spinning around and around on the rim.

And then I heard Andro: *Oops! We don't win unless it goes in the* other *basket, right?* And suddenly the ball spun away from the basket and flew to the other end of the court and into the basket there.

"Hennerly scored for us!" one of the kids on our team shouted.

"*I* didn't do that!" Hennerly said.

Then the coach said, "I think it's time to end this game. Funniest wind I ever saw inside a gymnasium."

And that was the game. I have been in a few basketball games and made some nutty throws. But this one was crazy!

But we didn't think about that for long.

Because we heard this voice. Everybody heard it.

"But I cannot see why," it said. "Give me one good reason why!"

And we looked, and there was Mr. Elbauer. He was standing in the doorway that led outside, and there was a dog alongside him. And Mr. Elbauer was shouting at it: "I don't *have* to give you a reason! Dogs are *not* permitted in the gym!"

Arguing with Andro

"Have you ever looked at the world as a dog does?" Andro said as we walked home and he trotted alongside me.

I was thinking, and I didn't feel like talking. But he kept on all by himself.

"They have a marvelous outlook on life," he said. "Have you ever noticed that? They see everything as a splendid game to be played. And they have great confidence. That's very important, you know."

"Andro," I said—I stopped. I didn't want to be seen arguing with a dog. Andro, I thought, you've got to stay away from the play tonight. I'll admit the basketball game was fun. It didn't matter that much, really. But the play is different. Three hundred people will be there watching. If you mess that up, I don't want to think what will happen.

"There is absolutely nothing to worry about. I'm simply going to watch, that's all. What could be more innocent?"

It was pretty easy to tell that he was going to the play, whether I liked it or not. So I gave up.

I didn't say much for the rest of the way home. I just listened to Andro, who kept talking about the trees on earth and the leaves that were turning and the color of the sky.

When we got home, he said, "I'll just think on up to your room and rest a bit, perhaps diagonally. Have you ever rested diagonally? It's quite soothing. I'll change myself into human form and show you. You simply lean to the side like this, until your body is halfway to the ground. And then you stop and rest. See how peaceful I look?"

He was leaning over to the side, and he was looking rested, I have to admit, and his eyes were closed, and there was a smile on his face.

"Jefferson?" said my father, "is that you?" He was in the garage. "Who's that with you? And what is he doing standing like that?"

As usual, it was crazy. Here I was, standing in my front yard with a man who was resting, leaning over sideways, halfway to the ground with a smile on his face.

My father came out into the front yard, but before he got there, Andro was gone. "Oh!" he said. "I thought there was someone with you."

"Probably the wind," I said.

"The wind?"

"Yeah. There's been a funny wind today." I grinned. "Hennerly made a great basket for our side. Only he was on the other team."

"You'd better come in," he said. "Maybe you should lie down before dinner."

I didn't lie down, though. I went up to

my room and argued with Andro, because I had been thinking.

"It is a bad idea for you to go to the play tonight," I said, "because you'll mess up everything. And it's a really important play to me. I want to be good in it. And it's not easy to act if somebody is always talking to you in your head or if he is floating around the ceiling or having an argument with Mr. Elbauer in the form of a dog."

"Oh, dear," Andro said. "I think I've upset you. I can't imagine how."

"That's what I mean," I said. "You don't think you're doing anything wrong, but earth people just don't look at things the way you do."

"Yes, I've noticed that."

"Okay. Then you won't go, right?"

"I wouldn't miss it for the world. But I promise you that during your play, I will appear only in my human form. I will be normal. Most. It will be quite exciting! I'll take thousands of notes."

"All right," I said. "You can go, since I can't stop you anyway."

"After the play, you shall see me no more," he said. "My ship arrives to pick me up at precisely nine thirty-seven tonight. I told them nine thirty-seven on the dot. Do you know why? Because your play will be over at exactly nine twenty-two."

I didn't ask him how he knew that. I wouldn't have understood the answer anyway. "I'd better go downstairs and get something to eat," I said. "I have to leave in fifteen minutes to get ready for the play."

"You'll be quite good," he said, "and you won't forget a single one of your lines."

"Right," I said. "How could I?"

"That's the spirit!"

And I went downstairs and got something to eat. I wondered why he had mentioned my lines when he knew that I didn't have any.

10

Stop the Play!

It was getting late, so I asked my dad to start the car. I ran up to my room and got a coat. "I have to drive to school with my father," I told Andro. "You'd better think on in. Unless maybe you've changed your mind about going."

"Not for the world," Andro said. "Are you sure you'll be all right in the car? Cars are so dangerous on earth. Thinking is a much safer way to travel, you know. We do run into each other occasionally, of course, but there's very little harm done."

"Still," I said, "I'd better go with my dad. Otherwise he'd want to know how I was going to get there."

"That's a very good point," Andro said.

And as we drove into town, I wondered

if Andro was going to forget and do something really horrible during the play.

I might have known he was. But after I got to school, I forgot about that. I was too busy getting ready for the play and putting on my costume. I wanted to do it right, even though I was only a member of the crowd. So I took a lot of care. It's a good thing I did, as it turned out.

There was a good audience for the play. Everybody's parents came. Things went pretty well for a while. The technical stuff was going okay. Most of the lights came on when they were supposed to, and the set didn't fall over, like it did last year. Hennerly was actually pretty good. He was so mad at me on account of the basketball game that he wasn't about to be shown up again.

In fact, hardly anything went wrong at all until near the end of the play.

The story is about this guy who gets into this argument with his wife and goes into the mountains about two hundred years ago. He falls asleep there and sleeps for twenty years. Then he comes back after the twenty years and goes into the town square. But nobody recognizes him. And he hardly recognizes his own daughter.

The play was almost over, and Jimbo was playing Rip van Winkle, the guy who went into the mountains. It was the scene where he comes back. Jimbo had on a white beard that went all the way to the floor, and all of us who were playing the townpeople were waiting to come onstage.

So Jimbo walked on the stage with his beard and went up to Jill Wilkons, who was playing his daughter, and said, "Daughter, it's me! I'm your father from long ago."

She started to back away from him, because she wasn't supposed to recognize him. And then all of the townspeople came running on, and we were shouting: "Who is this man? We've never seen him before!"

And Jill said, "But how can you be my father when I don't know you?"

Then Hennerly, who played Jill's husband, went up to the old man and said, "You better get out of town. And now!" And all the townspeople started yelling at him to leave.

And then on top of all the shouting, we heard a voice, and it was Andro's. He was saying: "Stop!" And I thought: Oh, no!

I looked around to see if maybe Andro was a dog again, arguing with Mr. Elbauer, but he wasn't. And he wasn't floating around the ceiling. He was coming down the aisle of the auditorium, looking just like Andro. He was saying, "This is going wrong! You don't know who this man is! You must not drive him out of town! I simply cannot permit it!"

Andro thought it was real! And now I was thinking fast, hoping I could get through to Andro: Andro, this is crazy! It isn't real, Andro! Andro! It isn't real! It's just a story!

But Andro didn't seem to hear. He walked right up on the stage and started telling all the townspeople that Rip van

Winkle had been asleep for twenty years and had grown twenty years older. That was why no one recognized him.

Then he turned to Hennerly and told him that he never should have said such a cruel thing to old Rip, who was really a good man, and everyone should be glad to see him back.

Now, the audience was a little surprised. They couldn't tell if this was supposed to happen or not.

On the stage, though, it was more like panic. Everyone was talking at once. Hennerly stood there, wide-eyed, not knowing *what* to do. The kids playing the townspeople were looking at one another, saying things like, "How did *this* happen?"

The whole thing, in fact, looked like it was going to turn into a disaster. Jill—Rip's daughter—left all the confusion and walked to the front of the stage. She said to the audience: "I don't know what's going on!" And that didn't help any.

"Mercy is a precious thing throughout

the entire universe," Andro was saying. He pointed to Jimbo. "This feeble old man must be welcomed home." And Jimbo was staring, with his mouth open. The kids in the crowd were saying, "What do we do now?" And I was whispering: "Try to act! Act as if it was part of the play."

Andro kept talking, but everybody else was talking now too. I looked at him. His mouth was going, but no one could hear a thing that he said—or that anyone else said, either.

Somebody had to do something. So I pushed my way out of the crowd and shouted: "Quiet! This man must be heard!" And suddenly there wasn't a sound.

Now everybody thought I was crazy, too.

"Ladies and gentlemen of the town," I said, "this man is not an ordinary person. In fact, he is pretty nutty, as anyone can see. But that doesn't mean we shouldn't listen to him. He must be heard."

"Quite right," said Andro. And he went to the edge of the stage and pointed to a

man in the front row. "You, sir," he said. "Go fetch the police. This pathetic old man must not be driven from the town."

"No, no!" I said. "That won't be necessary. This is a democracy. We will decide it ourselves."

Andro turned to me. "But these people are trying to send a poor man away from his own home." And he pointed to Hennerly, who was standing at the side of the stage. "This evil man," Andro said, "should be made to vanish from the face of Albos. No. I am not on Albos. Earth, I mean."

I glanced over at Hennerly, who was looking around for a way to get out of there.

I ran to Andro. "You don't understand!"

"Oh, I think I do," he said. And then he did something I have thought a lot about since. He winked at me!

That rattled me. But only for a moment. I turned to the crowd. "Folks, this man has made a point. We in the crowd must agree with him. The old man must be given a chance. We must hear his side of the story."

"Splendidly put, indeed," Andro said. And he walked off the stage.

And everybody breathed easy. Because just at the moment that Andro had come down the aisle, Hennerly was supposed to say to Rip: "You, sir. Explain who you are!" And Hennerly looked at me, and I nodded quickly, and that is exactly what he said. And all of us in the crowd grinned, and the play went on. And it got over, too!

After the curtain closed, everybody on the stage was talking all at once and patting me on the back and saying that what I did really took fast thinking. But I said anybody could have done it if they thought they could.

My mother and father came on the stage. My dad said, "I knew you had it in you."

Then Mrs. Martinez, the director, came running up to me and threw her arms around me. She hugged me so hard that I could barely breathe. "You saved it!" she

said. "You saved it with the fastest thinking I have ever seen on a stage!" And she
hugged me again. "You're beautiful!" she
said.

Imagine that? Who ever said I was beautiful?

11

Starting Over

Everybody was leaving the stage to get out of costume. I started to follow them. Then I noticed the clock on the stage wall. It was nine twenty-seven. Andro's ship was coming back at nine thirty-seven. He would be gone—probably forever—in ten minutes!

I ran out into the auditorium and looked all around, but I didn't see him. My parents were there and a few other people. Mr. Elbauer was at the door talking with a police officer. Andro was gone.

I ran into the lobby. He wasn't there either. I came back and stood by Mr. Elbauer and the police officer, waiting to ask if they had seen him. But I never got the chance.

"I'm terribly sorry," the officer was saying, "but rules are rules."

"I *make* the rules!" Mr. Elbauer said. "Now let me go. There has been a disturbance here, and I was called, and I intend to get to the bottom of it."

"You must lower your voice," the officer said, "or I shall be forced to call the wagon."

"Wagon!" shouted Mr. Elbauer. "How dare you!"

The officer looked at me. "I think," he said, "that it is time to handcuff this man and take him away. Won't that be splendid?"

Oh, no! I thought.

And the officer smiled at me.

"I'd better get out of costume," I said. "A friend of mine is leaving in a few minutes."

The officer turned to Mr. Elbauer. "Will you excuse me for a moment? It'll only be a minute, and then we'll be off to jail. Won't that be nice?" He turned and took my hand. "You were quite good. Plays are very interesting."

"Jail!" said Mr. Elbauer.

"Now, my boy," Andro said to me, "you go on home, and I'll meet you there, and you can watch me leave."

"What do you mean, jail?" Mr. Elbauer said. And he began shouting that he was *not* going to jail. Andro turned to him and said that he was, too, going to jail, and they got into this big argument all over again.

At the same time that Andro was arguing with Mr. Elbauer at the top of his lungs, I heard him in my head, as calm as anything, saying, *Now, you just get out of your costume and go home. I'll be along soon. There's plenty of time. My ship won't arrive until nine seventy-three.*

I thought back: No, you have it mixed up. You mean nine thirty-seven.

No. I'm sure it's nine seventy-three.

But we don't *have* a nine seventy-three.

You don't? That's odd. Why not?

I don't know. I'll ask tomorrow. Anyway, you'll meet me in my room?

Of course.

Good, I thought. I ran off. As I left the auditorium, I could hear Andro saying to Mr. Elbauer: "If you do not come along quietly, I shall be forced to write you up in my forms, and do you know what *that* means?"

I left. And I was feeling pretty good. Things started to look different, all of a sudden. I was kind of proud of myself for what I had done in the play. No one else had been able to save the play but me. Not even Hennerly.

I thought about school and how I was probably the lousiest student there. But Andro had been in my class, and he liked it a lot. He did admit that English was a little boring. He liked what he learned about Champlain. But he said that when Mrs. Luff explained the historical background, he had—even with his great mind—fallen asleep a couple of times.

I got out of costume, and we drove home. When we got there, I said good night to my mom and dad. They were feeling pretty good about how I had become the big guy at the play. So was I.

When I got up to my room, Andro was staring out the window. "Well," he said, "the day went splendidly, don't you think?"

I smiled. "Quite splendid," I said.

He turned to me. "You have a marvelous planet here. Somewhat complicated, as planets go, but certainly intriguing. I must say, I enjoyed myself."

And then the glow started to come in. I could see it way up in the sky, and it was heading for the same place in the field where I first saw Andro.

Andro told me his trip to earth had been so interesting that he had forgotten to make notes on his forms. He said that back home they'd be pretty mad about that, but he would take twice as many notes on the next planet.

And then he said good-bye and patted me on the back. The next thing I knew, he was gone.

I felt kind of alone. I guess I had been hoping that he was going to be here forever, doing my homework and helping me in basketball. So I said to myself: "Okay, Jefferson, open up that math book and do the problems yourself."

I opened the book, all right, and I turned to the exercises, but I couldn't understand the *questions*, let alone answer them. So I said, "Okay, back to the beginning." And I started at the front of the book. When the sun came up the next morning, I was just getting to the exercises that were due that day. I did them, and they weren't as hard as I thought.

I ate breakfast and walked to school, whistling all the way and feeling great, even though I hadn't slept at all.

At school, everybody congratulated me about the play. It seemed as if everyone in the world had heard about it. I went to class and listened to Mrs. Luff talk about history—and I will tell you that you can only do that if you *think* you can.

Hennerly was sitting there in class, as he always was, but he wasn't looking as superior as he usually did. I guess the play shook him a little. And I figured he's probably not a bad guy, really. If he gets shook up once in a while, he's probably even human, which had not occurred to me before.

Anyway, when Mrs. Luff called on me, I gave her the right answer.

Mrs. Luff, who was getting ready to call on somebody else, because she figured my answer would be wrong, as usual, stopped. "Where did you get that?" she said.

"From my homework," I said. "I worked the problem."

"All right," she said. "I'll accept that. Please work it out on the board."

And I did. And that, I will tell you, stopped everybody.

And that's how things have been going ever since Andro left. I get quite a few good parts in plays now. So does Hennerly, and he is actually not too bad. I have been telling him that you can do whatever you want to, as long as you think you can.

JOIN IN THE FUN AND ADVENTURE WITH

BY NATALIE STANDIFORD

SPACE DOG AND ROY   75953-5/$2.95 US/$3.50 Can

When a spaceship crashes in his backyard, Roy gets what he's always wanted—a dog of his very own. But Space Dog is no ordinary pet, he's an explorer from the planet Queekrg on a secret mission to study Earth.

SPACE DOG AND THE PET SHOW   75954-3/$2.95 US/$3.50 Can

Roy wants the whole world to know that Space Dog is special. Space Dog can walk, talk and count, and Roy thinks winning a ribbon at the pet show is a sure thing.

SPACE DOG IN TROUBLE   75955-1/$2.95 US/$3.50 Can

While trying to escape the disgusting, slobbery Blanche, Space Dog runs smack into the dog catcher and ends up spending a night in the pound.

SPACE DOG THE HERO   75956-X/$2.95 US/$3.50 Can

After a burglary in the neighborhood, Roy's dad insists that Space Dog guard the house. Space Dog can do a lot of things—like talk and spell—but scaring away robbers isn't one of them.

JOIN TWIN DETECTIVES MICKEY AND KATE IN ALL THEIR ADVENTURES

Swing into reading with Marion M. Markham's delightful books!

THE HALLOWEEN CANDY MYSTERY
Twins Mickey and Kate begin their detective career right next door. #0-380-70965-1 $2.95 US ($3.50 Canada)

THE BIRTHDAY PARTY MYSTERY
Someone is spoiling Debbie Allen's birthday party at the local zoo. #0-380-70968-6 $2.95 US ($3.50 Canada)

THE THANKSGIVING DAY PARADE MYSTERY
The Springvale Marching Band is missing—and someone has broken into the bank.
#0-380-70967-8 $2.95 US ($3.50 Canada)

THE CHRISTMAS PRESENT MYSTERY
Mickey and Kate's favorite uncle is in for a surprise when he opens the gift the twins have prepared.
#0-380-70966-X $2.95 US ($3.50 Canada)

Avon Camelot Presents Fantabulous Fun from Mike Thaler, America's "Riddle King"

FRANKENSTEIN'S PANTYHOSE
75613-7 $2.50 US/$2.95 Can

CREAM OF CREATURE FROM THE SCHOOL CAFETERIA
89862-4 $2.50 US/$3.25 Can

A HIPPOPOTAMUS ATE THE TEACHER
78048-8 $2.95 US/$3.50 Can

KING KONG'S UNDERWEAR
89823-3 $2.50 US/$2.95 Can

THERE'S A HIPPOPOTAMUS UNDER MY BED
40238-6 $2.50 US/$3.50 Can

UPSIDE DOWN DAY
89999-X $2.50 US/$2.95 Can

Look for More Mystery Adventure
And Fun in the Kitchen With

Cookie McCorkle...

AND THE CASE OF THE
  EMERALD EARRINGS
                    76098-3/$2.95 US/$3.50 Can

AND THE CASE OF THE
  KING'S GHOST
                    76350-8/$2.99 US/$3.50 Can

AND THE CASE OF THE
  MISSING CASTLE
                    76348-6/$2.99 US/$3.50 Can

AND THE CASE OF THE
  POLKA-DOT SAFECRACKER
                    76099-1/$2.95 US/$3.50 Can

Each Book Includes Easy-to-Follow Recipes
For Cookie's Favorite Dishes!